PUFFIN BOOKS

Editor: Kaye Webb

The Young Puffin Book of Verse

This is a collection of poems, verses, nursery rhymes and jingles for children up to the age of eight. It is an introduction to a vast heritage of poetry. Though diverse in form, language, mood and subject, each poem has been chosen with care as being within the grasp of young readers and listeners.

The collection spans continents as well as centuries. Fifty-six poets are represented, including a number from America. Readers will find here poems by writers whose names are bywords in the world of children's literature: Edward Lear, Kate Greenaway and Walter de la Mare, as well as many poems by writers whose names are normally found only in collections for adults: Robert Frost, W. B. Yeats, James Kirkup. All the poets with whom modern children are familiar are here too, including James Reeves, Rachel Field, Eleanor Farjeon and Leonard Clark. Finally, there are also many anonymous poems.

It is my hope that children will enjoy the liveliness of the book and this will be the beginning of a lifetime's appreciation of poetry, and that parents will derive a twofold pleasure: that of sharing with their children poems they learned at a similar age and of discovering and exploring verse by contemporary English and American poets, many of whom write especially for children.

BARBARA IRESON

ILLUSTRATED BY
Gioia Fiammenghi

The Young Puffin
Book of Verse

COMPILED
FOR PUFFIN BOOKS BY
Barbara Ireson

PUFFIN BOOKS

Puffin Books, Penguin Books Ltd, Harmondsworth, Middlesex, England
Penguin Books Inc., 7110 Ambassador Road, Baltimore, Maryland 21207, U.S.A.
Penguin Books Australia Ltd, Ringwood, Victoria, Australia
Penguin Books Canada Ltd, 41 Steelcase Road West, Markham, Ontario, Canada
Penguin Books (N.Z.) Ltd, 182–190 Wairau Road, Auckland 10, New Zealand

—

First published 1970
Reprinted 1970, 1971, 1972, 1973, 1974, 1975 (twice)

—

Copyright © Barbara Ireson, 1970

—

Made and printed in Great Britain
by Richard Clay (The Chaucer Press) Ltd,
Bungay, Suffolk
Set in Monotype Bembo

Contents

Acknowledgements

The editor and publishers wish to thank the following for permission to use copyright material in this collection:

Abelard–Schuman for *As fit as a fiddle, My name is . . .* and *I Spy* by Pauline Clarke from *Silver Bells and Cockle Shells*, and *A Spike of Green* by Barbara Baker from *Poems and Pictures*; Angus and Robertson Ltd for *The Barber* and *The Porter* by C. J. Dennis from *A Book for Kids*; Atheneum Publishers for *Until I saw the Sea* and *Mine*, text copyright © 1967 by Lilian Moore, from *I Feel the Same Way*; Basil Blackwell, Oxford, for *Little Girl, The Family* and *Dancing Game* by Rose Fyleman from *Widdy-Widdy-Wurkey*, and *Wanted*; The Bodley Head Ltd for *Jack Frost* by Gabriel Setoun from *The Child World*; Brockhampton Press for *Johnny's Pockets* by Alison Winn from *Helter Skelter* and *Tea with Me* from *Roundabout*; Brandt & Brandt for *When I grow up* by William Wise from *Jonathan Blake*, published by Alfred A. Knopf, New York; Collins Publishers and Harcourt Brace Jovanovich Inc. for *If I Were Teeny Tiny* and *Sing a Song of Pockets* by Beatrice Schenk de Regniers from *Something Special*, © by Beatrice Schenk de Regniers; Collier-Macmillan Ltd for *The Bullfrog's Song* and *If I Could Have a Pair of Wings* by Anita E. Posey from *Rings and Things*; Ian Colvin for *The Nightingale* from *Rhyme and Rhythm* published by Macmillan; Curtis Brown Ltd and Little Brown & Company for *Winter Morning* and *The Swallow* copyright © 1961, 1962 by Ogden Nash, *Camel* and *Unicorn* by

and the Fox and Mice and Cat by Clive Sansom from The Golden Unicorn; Methuen and E. P. Dutton & Co. Inc. for In the Fashion, Puppy and I, Rice Pudding and The Four Friends by A. A. Milne from When We Were Very Young; the Estate of Mildred Plew Meigs for Johnny Fife and Johnny's Wife; Mary Britton Miller for Cat from Fresh Flights; Jessica Nelson North for A Long Story; Oxford University Press for The Lonely Scarecrow by James Kirkup from Refusal to Conform; Laurence Pollinger Ltd and Holt, Rinehart and Winston Inc., for The Last Word of a Bluebird as told to a Child from The Poetry of Robert Frost, edited by E. C. Lathem, published by Jonathan Cape Ltd, copyright 1916, © 1969 Holt, Rinehart and Winston Inc. © 1944 by Robert Frost; Scott, Foresman & Company for Noses, My Puppy, Upside Down and Teddy Bear by Aileen Fisher from Up the Windy Hill published by Abelard-Schuman, London, and Scott, Foresman & Co., Glenview, Illinois; Charles Scribner's Sons for August Afternoon from Open the Door (copyright 1949 Marion Edey and Dorothy Grider); Hal Summers for Leaves in the Yard; The Viking Press Inc. for The Rabbit by Elizabeth Madox Roberts from Under the Tree, copyright 1922 B. W. Huebsch Inc. 1950 Ivor S. Roberts; Frederick Warne & Co. for The Old Woman by Beatrix Potter from Appley Dapply's Nursery Rhymes; Mrs Iris Wise, Macmillan & Co Ltd London and Canada, and The Macmillan Co. New York for The Rivals from Collected Poems of James Stephens; World's Work and Doubleday & Co. Inc. for Meeting, The Pet Shop and General Store by Rachel Field, from Taxis and Toadstools; M. B. Yeats, Macmillan & Co. Ltd and The Macmillan Co., New York, for To a Squirrel at Kyle-na-no from Collected Poems of W. B. Yeats, copyright 1919 by The Macmillan Co., © renewed 1947 by Bertha Georgia Yeats. If is taken from The Mother Goose Treasury published by Hamish Hamilton, based on versions of old rhymes collected by Peter and Iona Opie.

Every effort has been made to trace copyright but if any omissions have been made please let us know in order that we may put it right in the next edition.

1

I Will Build you a House

Little Girl

I WILL build you a house
If you do not cry,
A house, little girl,
As tall as the sky.

I will build you a house
Of golden dates,
The freshest of all
For the steps and gates.

I will furnish the house,
For you and for me
With walnuts and hazels
Fresh from the tree.

I will build you a house,
And when it is done
I will roof it with grapes
To keep out the sun.

ROSE FYLEMAN
from an Arabian nursery rhyme

An Old Woman of the Roads

O, TO have a little house!
   To own the hearth and stool and all!
The heaped-up sods upon the fire,
   The pile of turf against the wall!

To have a clock with weights and chains
   And pendulum swinging up and down!
A dresser filled with shining delph,
   Speckled and white and blue and brown!

I could be busy all the day
   Clearing and sweeping hearth and floor,
And fixing on their shelf again
   My white and blue and speckled store!

I could be quiet there at night
   Beside the fire and by myself,
Sure of a bed, and loth to leave
   The ticking clock and the shining delph!

Och! but I'm weary of mist and dark,
    And roads where there's never a house or bush,
And tired I am of bog and road
    And the crying wind and the lonesome hush!

And I am praying to God on high,
    And I am praying Him night and day,
For a little house – a house of my own –
    Out of the wind's and the rain's way.

PADRAIC COLUM

Houses

I LIKE old houses best, don't you?
They never go cluttering up a view
With roofs too red and paint too new,
With doors too green and blinds too blue!
The old ones look as if they *grew*,
Their bricks may be dingy, their clapboards askew
From sitting so many seasons through,
But they've learned in a hundred years or two
Not to go cluttering up a view!

RACHEL FIELD

House Coming Down

THEY'RE pulling down the house
  At the corner of the Square,
The floors and the ceilings
  Are out in the air,
The fireplaces so rusty,
The staircases so dusty,
And wallpaper so musty,
  Are all laid bare.

It looks like a dollshouse
  With the dolls put away,
And the furniture laid by
  Against another day;
No bed to lie in,
No pan to fry in,
Or dish to make a pie in,
  And nobody to play.

That was the parlour
  With the cream-and-yellow scrawls,
That was the bedroom
  With the roses on the walls,
There's a dark red lining
In the room they had for dining,
And a brown one, rather shining,
  Goes all up the halls.

But where is the lady
In a pretty gown?
Where is the baby
That used to crow and frown?
Oh, the rooms look so little,
The house looks so brittle,
And no one cares a tittle
If it all tumbles down.

ELEANOR FARJEON

Wanted

I'M looking for a house
Said the little brown mouse,
with
One room for breakfast,
One room for tea,
One room for supper,
And that makes three.

One room to dance in,
When I give a ball,
A kitchen and a bedroom,
Six rooms in all.

ROSE FYLEMAN

The Cold Old House

I KNOW a house, and a cold old house,
  A cold old house by the sea.
If I were a mouse in that cold old house
  What a cold cold mouse I'd be!

ANON.

The Deserted House

THERE'S no smoke in the chimney,
  And the rain beats on the floor;
There's no glass in the window,
  There's no wood in the door;
The heather grows behind the house,
  And the sand lies before.

No hand hath trained the ivy,
  The walls are grey and bare;
The boats upon the sea sail by,
  Nor ever tarry there.
No beast of the field comes nigh,
  Nor any bird of the air.

MARY COLERIDGE

Johnny Fife and Johnny's Wife

Oh, Johnny Fife and Johnny's wife,
  To save their toes and heels,
They built themselves a little house
  That ran on rolling wheels.

They hung their parrot at the door
  Upon a painted ring,
And round and round the world they went
  And never missed a thing;

And when they wished to eat they ate,
  And after they had fed,
They crawled beneath a crazy quilt
  And gaily went to bed;

And what they cared to keep they kept,
  And what they both did not,
They poked beneath a picket fence
  And quietly forgot.

Oh, Johnny Fife and Johnny's wife,
  They took their brush and comb,
And round and round the world they went
  And also stayed at home.

MILDRED PLEW MEIGS

There was an old woman who lived in a shoe,
She had so many children she didn't know what to do;
She gave them some broth without any bread;
She whipped them all soundly and put them to bed.

ANON.

The Old Woman

You know the old woman
    Who lived in a shoe?
And had so many children
    She didn't know what to do?

I think if she lived in
    A little shoe-house –
That little old woman was
    Surely a mouse!

BEATRIX POTTER

THERE was an old woman called Nothing-at-all,
Who lived in a dwelling exceedingly small;
A man stretched his mouth to its utmost extent,
And down at one gulp house and old woman went.

ANON.

THERE was an old woman lived under a hill,
And if she's not gone, she lives there still,
Baked apples she sold, and cranberry pies,
And she's the old woman that never told lies.

ANON.

Mother Shuttle

OLD Mother Shuttle
Lived in a coal-scuttle,
Along with her dog and her cat;
What they ate I can't tell
But 'tis known very well,
That not one of the party was fat.

Old Mother Shuttle
Scoured out her coal-scuttle,
And washed both her dog and her cat;
The cat scratched her nose,
So they came to hard blows,
And who was the gainer by that?

ANON.

A Long Story

THERE was an old woman who lived in a house
And the house fell down on her head.
She took her twelve children up under her arms
And went to live in a shed.

The wind blew up and the wind blew down
And the children blew far and wide.
'Let us go and live in the haystack now!'
The cheerful old woman cried.

They lived in the haystack very well,
Six boys, six girls and the mother,
Till the hungry cows ate up their house
And they had to find another.

'We will live in a box by the side of the road!'
And this they proceeded to do,
Till a bonfire came and burned their box,
And they said, 'Let us live in a shoe!'

But the shoes were too small, and the heels were too
    tall,
And the toes were far too tight,
And they slept outdoors for weeks and weeks
Before they found one that was right.

A shoe so right, so roomy and bright,
It surely couldn't be true!
They made their kitchen in the heel
And slept in the toe of the shoe.

They slept in the toe where the wind couldn't blow,
Six boys and six girls in their beds.
And out of the holes where the lacings go
They stuck their wee little heads.

But every day the old woman would say
As she dusted and swept her floor,
'If the giant comes who wore this shoe
It won't be our house any more.'

The children played and were not afraid,
While the mother dusted and swept.
But a giant high, with his head in the sky,
Came by while the family slept.

'Why, here is my poor old shoe,' said he,
'That I lost a year ago.'
He picked it up and the children rolled
From their twelve little beds in the toe.

'We must lie very still so that none of us spill,'
Said the mother, 'whatever we do.'
The giant heard not even a word
As he started home with his shoe.

Six boys, six girls, the mother and all,
They came to the giant's street.
'I will put on my good old shoes,' said he,
'To comfort my poor old feet.'

Six boys, six girls, the mother and all
Lay still in the toe of their house,
The giant put in his foot and cried,
'A mouse, a terrible mouse!'

He ran away in a torrent of tears
And he never came back there, never!
And the old woman said, 'We will live here, my dears,
Forever and ever and ever.'

JESSICA NELSON NORTH

2

Sing a Song of People

Sing a Song of People

Sing a song of people
   Walking fast or slow;
People in the city,
   Up and down they go.

People on the sidewalk,
People on the bus;
People passing, passing,
In back and front of us.
People on the subway
Underneath the ground;
People riding taxis
Round and round and round.

People with their hats on,
Going in the doors;
People with umbrellas
When it rains and pours.
People in tall buildings
And in stores below;
Riding elevators
Up and down they go.

People walking singly,
People in a crowd;
People saying nothing,
People talking loud.
People laughing, smiling,
Grumpy people too;
People who just hurry
And never look at you!

Sing a song of people
    Who like to come and go;
Sing of city people
    You see but never know!

LOIS LENSKI

Wonders of Nature

My Grandmother said, 'Now isn't it queer,
That boys must whistle and girls must sing?
But that's how 'tis!' I heard her say –
'The same tomorrow as yesterday.'

Grandmother said, when I asked her why
Girls couldn't whistle the same as I,
'Son, you know it's a natural thing –
Boys just whistle, and girls just sing.'

ANON.

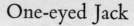

One-eyed Jack

ONE-EYED Jack, the pirate chief,
Was a terrible, fearsome ocean thief.
He wore a peg
Upon one leg;
He wore a hook –
And a dirty look!
One-eyed Jack, the pirate chief –
A terrible, fearsome ocean thief!

ANON.

Skipping

LITTLE children skip,
The rope so gaily gripping,
  Tom and Harry,
  Jane and Mary,
  Kate, Diana,
  Susan, Anna,
All are fond of skipping!

The grasshoppers all skip,
The early dew-drop sipping,
　Under, over
　Bent and clover,
　Daisy, sorrel,
　Without quarrel,
All are fond of skipping!

The little boats they skip,
Beside the heavy shipping,
　And while the squalling
　Winds are calling,
　Falling, rising,
　Rising, falling,
All are fond of skipping!

The autumn leaves they skip,
When blasts the trees are stripping;
　Bounding, whirling,
　Sweeping, twirling,
　And in wanton
　Mazes curling,
All are fond of skipping!

THOMAS HOOD

Looe

BIDDERLY-DO, bidderly-do,
I'm on a train and I'm off to Looe.
Ra-ta-ta-tar, ra-ta-ta-tar,
I'm going to visit my Grandmamma.
Tickety-tack, tickety-tack,
Into a tunnel that's ever so black.
A-rumpety-tum, a-rumpety-tum,
I'm taking a present to Granny from Mum.
Tickety-boo, tickety-boo,
I always enjoy the journey to Looe.
Chi-chi-chi-choo,
Chi-chi-chi. . . . . CHOO!

ROLAND EGAN

Johnny's Pockets

JOHNNY collects
Conkers on strings,
Sycamore seeds
With aeroplane wings,
Green acorn cups,
Seaweed and shells,
Treasures from crackers
Like whistles and bells.

Johnny collects
Buttons and rings,
Bits of a watch,
Cog wheels and springs,
Half-eaten sweets,
Nuts, nails and screws.
That's why his pockets
Bulge out of his trews.

ALISON WINN

Noses

I looked in the mirror
and looked at my nose:
it's the funniest thing,
the way it grows
stuck right out where all of it shows
with two little holes where the
                    breathing goes.

I looked in the mirror
and saw in there
the end of my chin
and the start of my hair
and between there isn't much space to spare
with my nose, like a handle, sticking there.

If ever you want
to giggle and shout
and can't think of what
to do it about,
just look in the mirror and then, no doubt,
you'll see how funny YOUR nose
                    sticks out!

AILEEN FISHER

The Window Cleaner

WHEN I grow up I want to be
A window cleaning man
And make the windows in our street
As shiny as I can.
I'll put my ladder by the wall
And up the steps I'll go
But when I'm up there with my pail
I hope the wind won't blow.

M. LONG

The Barber

I'D like to be a barber, and learn to shave and clip,
Calling out, 'Next, please!' and pocketing my tip.
All day you'd hear my scissors going, 'Snip, Snip,
    Snip!'
I'd lather people's faces, and their noses I would grip
While I shaved most carefully along the upper lip.
  But I wouldn't be a barber if . . .
    The razor was to slip.
      Would you?

C. J. DENNIS

The Milkman

CLINK, clink, clinkety clink.
The milkman's on his rounds, I think.
Crunch, crunch come the milkman's feet
Closer and closer along the street –
Then clink, clink, clinkety-clink,
He's left our bottles of milk to drink.

CLIVE SANSOM

The Porter

I'd like to be a porter, and always on the run,
Calling out, 'Stand aside!' and asking leave of none,
Shoving trucks on people's toes, and having splendid
      fun;
Slamming all the carriage doors and locking every one –
And, when they asked to be let in, I'd say, 'It can't be
      done.'
   But I wouldn't be a porter if . . .
      The luggage weighed a ton.
         Would you?

C. J. DENNIS

Jemima Jane

JEMIMA JANE,
  Oh, Jemima Jane,
She loved to go out
  And slosh in the rain.
She loved to go out
  And get herself wet,
And she had a duck
  For her favourite pet.

Every day
  At half-past four
They'd both run out
  The kitchen door;
They'd find a puddle,
  And there they'd stay
Until it was time
  To go away.

They got quite wet,
  But they didn't mind;
And every rainy
  Day they'd find
A new way to splash
  Or a new way to swim.
And the duck loved Jane,
  And Jane loved him.

MARCHETTE CHUTE

Jeremiah Obadiah

JEREMIAH OBADIAH
    puff, puff, puff,
When he gives his messages he
    snuffs, snuffs, snuffs,
When he goes to school by day he
    roars, roars, roars,
When he goes to bed at night he
    snores, snores, snores,
When he goes to Christmas treat he eats
    plum-duff,
Jeremiah Obadiah
    puff, puff, puff.

                  ANON.

Minnie

MINNIE can't make her mind up,
Minnie can't make up her mind!
  They ask her at tea,
  'Well, what shall it be?'
  And Minnie says, 'Oh,
  Muffins, please! no,
  Sandwiches – yes,
  Please, egg-and-cress –
  I mean a jam one,
  Or is there a ham one,
Or is there another kind?
  Never mind!
        Cake
  Is what I will take,
The sort with the citron-rind,
  Or p'r'aps the iced one –
  Or is there a spiced one,
Or is there the currant kind?'
  When tea is done
  She hasn't begun,
She's always the one behind,
Because she can't make her mind up,
Minnie can't make up her mind!

ELEANOR FARJEON

44

Rice Pudding

WHAT is the matter with Mary Jane?
She's crying with all her might and main,
And she won't eat her dinner – rice pudding again –
What *is* the matter with Mary Jane?

What is the matter with Mary Jane?
I've promised her dolls and a daisy-chain,
And a book about animals – all in vain –
What *is* the matter with Mary Jane?

What is the matter with Mary Jane?
She's perfectly well, and she hasn't a pain;
But, look at her, now she's beginning again! –
What *is* the matter with Mary Jane?

What is the matter with Mary Jane?
I've promised her sweets and a ride in the train,
And I've begged her to stop for a bit and explain –
What *is* the matter with Mary Jane?

What is the matter with Mary Jane?
She's perfectly well and she hasn't a pain,
And it's lovely rice pudding for dinner again! –
What *is* the matter with Mary Jane?

A. A. MILNE

Bedtime

FIVE minutes, five minutes more, please!
  Let me stay five minutes more!
Can't I just finish the castle
  I'm building here on the floor?
Can't I just finish the story
  I'm reading here in my book?
Can't I just finish this bead-chain –
  It *almost* is finished, look!
Can't I just finish this game, please?
  When a game's once begun
It's a pity never to find out
  Whether you've lost or won.
Can't I just stay five minutes?
  Well, can't I stay just four?
Three minutes, then? two minutes?
  Can't I stay *one* minute more?

ELEANOR FARJEON

Grandma

GRANDMA's gone a-visiting,
A-visiting today;
Put on her gown that's flowered and silky,
'And now,' says she, 'the girls must milky,
The serving-maid must meat the pig,
The little lad bring round the gig,
For I'm going a-visiting,
A-visiting all day.'

Grandpa's home a-worrying,
A-worrying today;
'Though missus be a treasure, she
Is over fond of pleasury,'
Says he, 'these flighty ways don't do
In women folk of seventy-two,'
So grandpa's home a-worrying,
A-worrying all day.

RUTH MANNING-SANDERS

As Fit as a Fiddle

GRANDFATHER GEORGE is as fit as a fiddle,
As fit as a fiddle right up from his middle,
Grandfather George is as fit as a fiddle,
As fit as a fiddle right down to his toes.

Grandfather George, whenever I meet him
Nips my right ear and asks me a riddle,
And when Mother questions him how he is keeping,
He slaps his left leg and says 'Fit as a fiddle!'

Once I said 'Grandfather George, why a fiddle,
Why is a fiddle especially fit?'
He laughed very loud and said 'Hey diddle-diddle,
I'll give you a sixpence if you'll answer that!'

So now I ask everyone, friends and relations,
People I talk to wherever I go,
I ask them on buses, in shops and at stations:
I suppose, by the way, that you do not know?

PAULINE CLARKE

John Mouldy

I SPIED John Mouldy in his cellar,
Deep down twenty steps of stone;
In the dusk he sat a-smiling,
　Smiling there alone.

He read no book, he snuffed no candle;
The rats ran in, the rats ran out;
And far and near, the drip of water
　Went whisp'ring about.

The dusk was still, with dew a-falling,
I saw the Dog-star bleak and grim,
I saw a slim brown rat of Norway
　Creep over him.

I spied John Mouldy in his cellar,
Deep down twenty steps of stone;
In the dusk he sat a-smiling,
　Smiling there alone.

WALTER DE LA MARE

Rich Man

I SAW a Rich Man walking down the street
With a chain across his waistcoat and spats on his feet,
With silver in his pockets that jingled as he walked,
And a solid gold tooth that gleamed when he talked.
He walked by the girls with their baskets on their knees
Full of white clove pinks and pink sweet peas,
He walked by the flower-girls whose baskets smelled
  like honey
With his face full of care and his mind full of money.

I saw the Rich Man, he never saw me,
So I see more than the Rich Man can see.

ELEANOR FARJEON

Washing Day

THE old woman must stand
   At the tub, tub, tub,
The dirty clothes
   To rub, rub, rub;
But when they are clean,
   And fit to be seen,
She'll dress like a lady,
   And dance on the green.

ANON.

3

Out of Doors

JANUARY cold desolate;
February all dripping wet;
March wind ranges;
April changes;
Birds sing in tune
    To flowers of May,
And sunny June
    Brings longest day;
In scorched July
The storm-clouds fly
Lightning-torn
August bears corn,
September fruit;
In rough October
Earth must disrobe her;
Stars fall and shoot
In keen November;
And night is long
And cold is strong
In bleak December.

CHRISTINA ROSSETTI

In the Rain

THERE is no colour in the rain
It's only water, wet and plain.
It makes damp spots upon my book
And splashes on my new dress, look!
But puddles, in the rainy weather,
Glisten like a peacock's feather.

RENÉ CLOKE

The Lonely Scarecrow

My poor old bones – I've only two –
A broomshank and a broken stave,
My ragged gloves are a disgrace,
My one peg-foot is in the grave.

I wear the labourer's old clothes;
Coat, shirt and trousers all undone.

I bear my cross upon a hill
In rain and shine, in snow and sun.

I cannot help the way I look.
My funny hat is full of hay.
– O, wild birds, come and nest in me!
Why do you always fly away?

JAMES KIRKUP

I Saw the Wind today

I saw the wind today:
I saw it in the pane
Of glass upon the wall:
A moving thing – 'twas like
No bird with widening wing,
No mouse that runs along
The meal bag under the beam.

I think it like a horse,
All black, with frightening mane,
That springs out of the earth,
And tramples on his way.
I saw it in the glass,
The shaking of a mane:
A horse that no one rides!

PADRAIC COLUM

The Wind

I CAN get through a doorway without any key,
And strip the leaves from the great oak tree.

I can drive storm-clouds and shake tall towers,
Or steal through a garden and not wake the flowers.

Seas I can move and ships I can sink;
I can carry a house-top or the scent of a pink.

When I am angry I can rave and riot;
And when I am spent, I lie quiet as quiet.

JAMES REEVES

Little Wind

LITTLE wind blow on the hill-top;
Little wind, blow down the plain;
Little wind, blow up the sunshine,
Little wind, blow off the rain.

KATE GREENAWAY

Spring

Now the sleeping creatures waken –
　　Waken, waken;
Blossoms with soft winds are shaken –
　　Shaken, shaken;
Squirrels scamper and the hare
Runs races which the children share
Till their shouting fills the air.

Now the woodland birds are singing –
　　Singing, singing;
Over field and orchard winging –
　　Winging, winging;
Swift and swallow unaware
Weave such beauty on the air
That the children hush and stare.

RAYMOND WILSON

THE days are clear,
  Day after day,
When April's here,
  That leads to May,
And June
Must follow soon:
  Stay, June, stay! —
If only we could stop the moon
And June!

CHRISTINA ROSSETTI

THERE is but one May in the year,
  And sometimes May is wet and cold;
There is but one May in the year
  Before the year grows old.

Yet though it be the chilliest May,
  With least of sun and most of showers,
Its wind and dew, its night and day,
  Bring up the flowers.

CHRISTINA ROSSETTI

A Spike of Green

WHEN I went out
The sun was hot,
It shone upon
My flower pot.

And there I saw
A spike of green
That no one else
Had ever seen!

On other days
The things I see
Are mostly old
Except for me.

But this green spike
So new and small
Had never yet
Been seen at all!

BARBARA BAKER

The River is a Piece of Sky

FROM the top of a bridge
The river below
Is a piece of sky –
     Until you throw
     A penny in
     Or a cockleshell
     Or a pebble or two
     Or a bicycle bell
     Or a cobblestone
     Or a fat man's cane –
And then you can see
It's a river again.

The difference you'll see
When you drop your penny:
The river has splashes,
The sky hasn't any.

JOHN CIARDI

Intruder

THE sun only scorches,
It doesn't watch; but the moon watches.
He peers down low at the earth
As we cross his path;
He fills the unmoving meadows
With white light and dark moon-shadows;
He stares into my room as far as he can reach,
Like a man with a large torch.

CLIVE SANSOM

August Afternoon

WHERE shall we go?
 What shall we play?
What shall we do
 On a hot summer day?

We'll sit in the swing.
 Go low. Go high.
And drink lemonade
 Till the glass is dry.

One straw for you,
 One straw for me,
In the cool green shade
 Of the walnut tree.

MARION EDEY AND
DOROTHY GRIDER

There are Big Waves

THERE are big waves and little waves,
Green waves and blue.
Waves you can jump over,
Waves you dive through,
Waves that rise up
Like a great water wall,
Waves that swell softly
And don't break at all,
Waves that can whisper,
Waves that can roar,
And tiny waves that run at you
Running on the shore.

ELEANOR FARJEON

Until I saw the Sea

UNTIL I saw the sea
I did not know
that wind
could wrinkle water so.

I never knew
that sun
could splinter a whole sea of blue.

Nor
did I know before,
a sea breathes in and out
upon a shore.

LILIAN MOORE

What is Pink?

WHAT is pink? a rose is pink
By the fountain's brink.
What is red? a poppy's red
In its barley bed.
What is blue? the sky is blue
Where the clouds float thro'
What is white? a swan is white
Sailing in the light.
What is yellow? pears are yellow,
Rich and ripe and mellow.
What is green? the grass is green,
With small flowers between.
What is violet? clouds are violet
In the summer twilight.
What is orange? why, an orange,
Just an orange!

CHRISTINA ROSSETTI

Beech Leaves

In autumn down the beechwood path
The leaves lie thick upon the ground.
It's there I love to kick my way
And hear the crisp and crashing sound.

I am a giant, and my steps
Echo and thunder to the sky.
How the small creatures of the woods
Must quake and cower as I go by!

This brave and merry noise I make
In summer also when I stride
Down to the shining, pebbly sea
And kick the frothing waves aside.

JAMES REEVES

Leaves in the Yard

LEAVES have the lightest footsteps
Of all who come in the yard.
They play rounders, they play tig,
They play no holds barred.

Late when people are all asleep
Still they scamper and weave.
They play robbers, they play cops,
They play adam and eve.

Tap, tap, on the pavement,
Flit, flit, in the air:
The sentry-going bat wonders what they're at,
The blank back-windows stare.

When they rest the wind rests,
When *they* go he goes too.
They play tiptoe, they play mouse,
He shouts *hoo*.

Summer, they fidgeted on trees:
Autumn called 'Enough!'
They play leapfrog, they play fights,
They play blind-man's-buff.

Ragged, swept in corners,
Fallen beyond recall,
Ragged and old, soon to be mould –
But light of heart wins all.

HAL SUMMERS

November the Fifth

AND you, big rocket,
  I watch how madly you fly
  Into the smokey sky
  With flaming tail;

Catherine wheel,
  I see how fiercely you spin
  Round and round on your pin;
  How I admire
  Your circle of fire.

Roman candle,
  I watch how prettily you spark
  Stars in the autumn dark
  Falling like rain
  To shoot up again.

And you, old guy,
   I see how sadly you blaze on
   Till every scrap is gone;
   Burnt into ashes
   Your skeleton crashes.

And so,
   The happy ending of the fun,
   Fireworks over, bonfire done;
   Must wait a year now to remember
   Another fifth of November.

LEONARD CLARK

Jack Frost

THE door was shut, as doors should be,
    Before you went to bed last night;
Yet Jack Frost has got in, you see,
    And left your window silver white.

He must have waited till you slept;
    And not a single word he spoke,
But pencilled o'er the panes and crept
    Away again before you woke.

And here are little boats, and there
    Big ships with sails spread to the breeze;
And yonder, palm trees waving fair
    On islands set in silver seas.

And butterflies with gauzy wings;
    And herds of cows and flocks of sheep;
And fruit and flowers and all the things
    You see when you are sound asleep.

And now you cannot see the hills
    Nor fields that stretch beyond the lane;
But there are fairer things than these
    His fingers traced on every pane.

Rocks and castles towering high;
  Hills and dales and streams and fields;
And knights in armour riding by,
  With nodding plumes and shining shields.

For creeping softly underneath
  The door when all the lights are out,
Jack Frost takes every breath you breathe,
  And knows the things you think about.

He paints them on the window pane
  In fairy lines with frozen steam;
And when you wake you see again
  The lovely things you saw in dream.

                    GABRIEL SETOUN

75

Winter Morning

WINTER is the king of showmen,
Turning tree stumps into snow men
And houses into birthday cakes
And spreading sugar over lakes.
Smooth and clean and frosty white,
The world looks good enough to bite.
That's the season to be young,
Catching snowflakes on your tongue.

Snow is snowy when it's snowing,
I'm sorry it's slushy when it's going.

OGDEN NASH

Snow

WHEN winter winds blow
Hedges to and fro
And the flapping crow
Has gone to his home long ago,
Then I know
Snow
Will quietly fall, grow
Overnight higher than houses below,
Stop the stream in its flow,
And so
In a few hours, show
Itself man's ancient foe.
O
How slow
Is the silent gathering of snow.

LEONARD CLARK

The last word of a bluebird
as told to a child

As I went out a Crow
In a low voice said, 'Oh,
I was looking for you.
How do you do?
I just came to tell you
To tell Lesley (will you?)
That her little Bluebird
Wanted me to bring word
That the north wind last night
That made the stars bright
And made ice on the trough
Almost made him cough
His tail feathers off.

He just had to fly!
But he sent her Good-bye,
And said to be good,
And wear her red hood,
And look for skunk tracks
In the snow with an axe –
And do everything!
And perhaps in the spring
He would come back and sing.'

ROBERT FROST

4

All the Animals

Hurt no living thing

HURT no living thing,
  Ladybird nor butterfly,
Nor moth with dusty wing,
Nor cricket chirping cheerily,
Nor grasshopper, so light of leap,
  Nor dancing gnat,
  Nor beetle fat,
Nor harmless worms that creep.

CHRISTINA ROSSETTI

My Puppy

It's funny
my puppy
knows just how I feel.

When I'm happy
he's yappy
and squirms like an eel.

When I'm grumpy
he's slumpy
and stays at my heel.

It's funny
my puppy
knows such a great deal.

AILEEN FISHER

A Little Talk

THE big brown hen and Mrs Duck
Went walking out together;
They talked about all sorts of things –
The farmyard, and the weather.
But all *I* heard was: 'Cluck!
    Cluck! Cluck!'
And 'Quack! Quack! Quack!'
    from Mrs Duck.

ANON.

Robbin-a-Bobbin

'WHAT are you doing there, Robbin-a-Bobbin,
  Under my window, out in the blue?'

'Building my nest, O Little One, Pretty One!
  Doing a thing that you cannot do!'

'What are you doing there, Robbin-a-Bobbin,
  Under my window, out in the blue?'

'Feeding my nestlings, Little One, Pretty One!
  Doing a thing that you cannot do!'

'What are you doing there, Little One, Pretty One!
  What are you doing? Tell me now, true!'

'Sewing my patch-work, Robbin-a-Bobbin!
  Doing a thing that you cannot do!'

LAURA RICHARDS

Upside down

IT's funny how beetles
and creatures like that
can walk upside down
as well as walk flat:

They crawl on a ceiling
and climb on a wall
without any practice
or trouble at all,

While I have been trying
for a year (maybe more)
and still I can't stand
with my head on the floor.

AILEEN FISHER

The Family

WIDDY-widdy-wurkey
Is the name of my turkey;
There-and-back again
Is the name of my hen;
Waggle-tail-loose
Is the name of my goose;
Widdy-widdy-wurkey
Is the name of my turkey.

Widdy-widdy-wurkey
Is the name of my turkey;
Quackery-quack
Is the name of my duck;
Grummelty-grig
Is the name of my pig;
Widdy-widdy-wurkey
Is the name of my turkey.

Widdy-widdy-wurkey
Is the name of my turkey;
Tinker-Tog
Is the name of my dog;
Velvety-pat
Is the name of my cat;
Widdy-widdy-wurkey
Is the name of my turkey.

Widdy-widdy-wurkey
Is the name of my turkey;
Fiery-speed
Is the name of my steed;
Run-of-the-house
Is the name of my mouse;
Widdy-widdy-wurkey
Is the name of my turkey.

Widdy-widdy-wurkey
Is the name of my turkey;
Very-well-done
Is the name of my son;
Dearer-than-life
Is the name of my wife;
Widdy-widdy-wurkey
Is the name of my turkey.

And now you know my famil*ee*
And all that does belong to me.

ROSE FYLEMAN

The Bullfrog's Song

THE bullfrog sang the strangest song;
　　He sang it night and day.
'Ker-runk, ker-runk! Ker-runk, ker-runk!'
　　Was all it seemed to say.
A duck who liked to sing thought he
　　Would give the song a try;
　　'Ker-runk!' 'Quack-Quack!'
　　'Ker-runk!' 'Quack-Quack!'
　　They sang as I walked by.

The spotted cow had never heard
　　A more delightful song;
Right then and there, the spotted cow
　　Began to sing along.
The frog, the duck, the spotted cow
　　Sang out so loud and clear,
　　'Ker-runk!' 'Quack-Quack!'
　　'Ker-runk!' 'Moo-Moo!'
　　Was all that I could hear.

The speckled hen, a mother hen,
  Whose work is never done,
Began to sing; for she knew when
  You sing, your work is fun.
The frog, the duck, the cow, the hen,
  All sang the happy song;
  'Ker-runk!' 'Quack-Quack!'
  'Moo-Moo!' 'Cluck-Cluck!'
They sang the whole day long.

        ANITA E. POSEY

The Mare

Look at the mare of Farmer Giles!
She's brushing her hooves on the mat;

Look at the mare of Farmer Giles!
She's knocked on the door, rat-a-tat!

With a clack of her hoof and a wave of her head
She's tucked herself up in the four-post bed,
And she's wearing the Farmer's hat!

HERBERT ASQUITH

The Caterpillar

BROWN and furry
Caterpillar in a hurry;
Take your walk
To the shady leaf or stalk.

May no toad spy you,
May the little birds pass by you;
Spin and die,
To live again a butterfly.

CHRISTINA ROSSETTI

The Swallow

FLY away, fly away, over the sea,
    Sun-loving swallow, for summer is done.
Come again, come again, come back to me,
    Bringing the summer and bringing the sun.

CHRISTINA ROSSETTI

The Rivals

I HEARD a bird at dawn
  Singing sweetly on a tree,
That the dew was on the lawn,
  And the wind was on the lea!
But I didn't listen to him,
  For he didn't sing to me!

I didn't listen to him,
  For he didn't sing to me
That the dew was on the lawn,
  And the wind was on the lea!
I was singing at the time
  Just as prettily as he!

I was singing all the time,
  Just as prettily as he,
About the dew upon the lawn,
  And the wind upon the lea!
So I didn't listen to him
  As he sang upon a tree!

JAMES STEPHENS

The Blackbird

In the far corner,
close by the swings,
every morning
a blackbird sings.

His bill's so yellow,
his coat's so black,
that he makes a fellow
whistle back.

Ann, my daughter,
thinks that he
sings for us two
especially.

HUMBERT WOLFE

The Nightingale

On his little twig of plum,
　His plum-tree twig, the nightingale
Dreamed one night that snow had come,
　On the hill and in the vale,
　In the vale and on the hill,
　Everything white and soft and still,
Only the snowflakes falling, falling,
　Only the snow . . .

On a night when the snow had come,
　As the snowflakes fell the nightingale
Dreamed of orchards white with plum,
　On the hill and in the vale,
　In the vale and on the hill,
　Everything white and soft and still,
Only the petals falling, falling,
　Only the plum . . .

IAN COLVIN

from a Japanese nursery rhyme

Robin's Song

ROBIN sang sweetly
    When the days were bright.
'Thanks! Thanks for Summer!'
    He sang with all his might.

Robin sang sweetly
    In the Autumn days:
'There are fruits for everyone.
    Let us all give praise!'

In the cold and wintry weather
    Still you hear his song.
'Somebody must sing,' said Robin,
    'Or Winter will seem long.'

When the Spring came back again,
    He sang, 'I told you so!
Keep on singing through the Winter;
    It will always go.'

ANON.

The Rabbit and the Fox

A RABBIT came hopping, hopping,
Hopping along in the park.
'I've just been shopping, shopping,
I must be home before dark.'

A fox came stalking, stalking,
Stalking from under a tree.
'Where are you walking, walking?
Why don't you walk with me?'

The rabbit went hopping, hopping,
Hopping away from the tree.
'I've just been shopping, shopping,
I must be home for my tea.'

'Come with me, bunny, bunny –
Bunny, you come with me;
I'll give you some honey, honey,
I'll give you some honey for tea.'

'I can't be stopping, stopping,
I'm far too busy today' –
And the rabbit went hopping, hopping,
Hopping away and away.

CLIVE SANSOM

The Rabbit

WHEN they said the time to hide was mine,
I hid back under a thick grape vine.

And while I was still for the time to pass,
A little grey thing came out of the grass.

He hopped his way through the melon bed
And sat down close by a cabbage head.

He sat down close where I could see,
And his big eyes still looked hard at me,

His big eyes bursting out of the rim,
And I looked back very hard at him.

ELIZABETH MADOX ROBERTS

The Donkey

I SAW a donkey
One day old,
His head was too big
For his neck to hold;
His legs were shaky
And long and loose,
They rocked and staggered
And weren't much use.

He tried to gambol
And frisk a bit,
But he wasn't quite sure
Of the trick of it.
His queer little coat
Was soft and grey,
And curled at his neck
In a lovely way.

His face was wistful
And left no doubt
That he felt life needed
Some thinking about.
So he blundered round
In venturesome quest,
And then lay flat
On the ground to rest.

He looked so little
And weak and slim,
I prayed the world
Might be good to him.

ANON.

Calling the Cows Home

'CUSHA! Cusha! Cusha!' calling,
For the dew will soon be falling,
Leave your meadow grasses mellow,
    Mellow, mellow!
Quit your cowslips, cowslips yellow,
Come up Whitefoot, come up Lightfoot,
Quit the stalks of parsley hollow,
    Hollow, hollow!
Come up Jetty, rise and follow,
From the clovers, lift your head.
Come up Whitefoot, come up Lightfoot,
Come up Jetty, rise and follow,
Jetty, to the milking shed.

JEAN INGELOW

Country Cat

'WHERE are you going, Mrs Cat,
All by your lonesome lone?'
'Hunting a mouse, or maybe a rat
Where the ditches are overgrown.'

'But you're very far from your house and home,
You've come a long, long way –'
'The further I wander, the longer I roam
The more I find mice at play.'

'But you're very near to the dark pinewood
And foxes go hunting too.'
'I know that a fox might find me good,
But what is a cat to do?'

'I have my kittens who must be fed,
I *can't* have them skin and bone!'
And Mrs Cat shook her brindled head
And went off by her lonesome lone.

ELIZABETH COATSWORTH

Cat

THE black cat yawns,
Opens her jaws,
Stretches her legs,
And shows her claws.

Then she gets up
And stands on four
Long stiff legs
And yawns some more.

She shows her sharp teeth,
She stretches her lip,
Her slice of a tongue
Turns up at the tip.

Lifting herself
On her delicate toes,
She arches her back
As high as it goes.

She lets herself down
With particular care,
And pads away
With her tail in the air.

MARY BRITTON MILLER

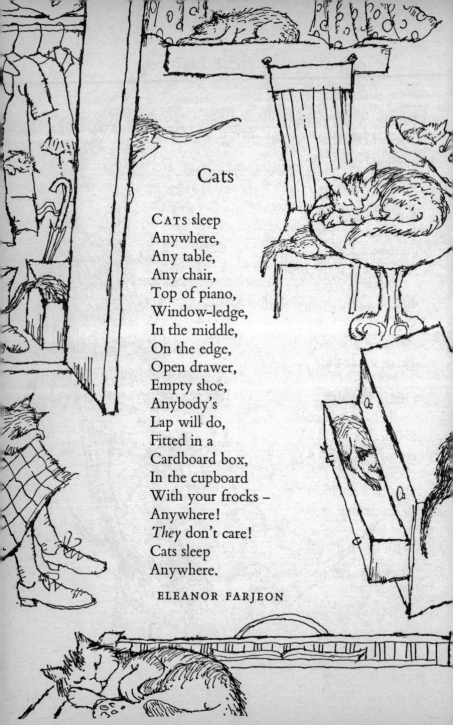

Cats

CATS sleep
Anywhere,
Any table,
Any chair,
Top of piano,
Window-ledge,
In the middle,
On the edge,
Open drawer,
Empty shoe,
Anybody's
Lap will do,
Fitted in a
Cardboard box,
In the cupboard
With your frocks –
Anywhere!
They don't care!
Cats sleep
Anywhere.

ELEANOR FARJEON

Choosing their Names

OUR old cat has kittens three –
What do you think their names should be?

One is tabby with emerald eyes,
    And a tail that's long and slender,
And into a temper she quickly flies
    If you ever by chance offend her.
        I think we shall call her this –
        I think we shall call her that –
Now, don't you think that Pepperpot
    Is a nice name for a cat?

One is black with a frill of white,
    And her feet are all white fur,
If you stroke her she carries her tail upright
    And quickly begins to purr.
        I think we shall call her this –
        I think we shall call her that –
Now, don't you think that Sootikin
    Is a nice name for a cat?

One is a tortoiseshell yellow and black,
    With plenty of white about him;
If you tease him, at once he sets up his back,
    He's a quarrelsome one, ne'er doubt him.
       I think we shall call him this –
       I think we shall call him that –
Now, don't you think that Scratchaway
       Is a nice name for a cat?

Our old cat has kittens three
And I fancy these their names will be:
Pepperpot, Sootikin. Scratchaway – there!
Were ever kittens with these to compare?
And we call the old mother –
       Now, what do you think? –
Tabitha Longclaws Tiddley Wink.

THOMAS HOOD

Sunning

OLD Dog lay in the summer sun
Much too lazy to rise and run.
He flapped an ear
At a buzzing fly;
He winked a half-opened
Sleepy eye;
He scratched himself
On an itching spot;
As he dozed on the porch
When the sun was hot.
He whimpered a bit
From force of habit,
While he lazily dreamed
Of chasing a rabbit.
But Old Dog happily lay in the sun,
Much too lazy to rise and run.

JAMES S. TIPPETT

To a Squirrel at Kyle-na-no

COME play with me;
Why should you run
Through the shaking tree
As though I'd a gun
To strike you dead?
When all I would do
Is to scratch your head
And let you go.

W. B. YEATS

Camel

THE Camel is a long-legged humpbacked beast
With the crumpled-up look of an old worn shoe.
He walks with a creep and a slouch and a slump
As over the desert he carries his hump
Like a top-heavy ship, like a bumper bump-bump.
See him plodding in caravans out of the East,
Bringing silk for a party and dates for a feast.
Is he tired? Is he *thirsty*? No, not in the least.
Good morning, Sir Camel! Good morning to you!

WILLIAM JAY SMITH

The Four Friends

ERNEST was an elephant, a great big fellow,
  Leonard was a lion with a six-foot tail,
George was a goat, and his beard was yellow,
  And James was a very small snail.

Leonard had a stall, and a great big strong one,
  Ernest had a manger, and its walls were thick,
George found a pen, but I think it was the wrong one,
  And James sat down on a brick.

Ernest started trumpeting, and cracked his manger,
  Leonard started roaring, and shivered his stall,
James gave the huffle of a snail in danger
  And nobody heard him at all.

Ernest started trumpeting and raised such a rumpus,
  Leonard started roaring and trying to kick,
James went a journey with the goat's new compass
  And he reached the end of his brick.

Ernest was an elephant and very well-intentioned,
  Leonard was a lion with a brave new tail,
George was a goat, as I think I have mentioned,
  But James was only a snail.

A. A. MILNE

Unicorn

THE Unicorn with the long white horn
  Is beautiful and wild.
He gallops across the forest green
So quickly that he's seldom seen
Where Peacocks their blue feathers preen
  And strawberries grow wild.
He flees the hunter and the hounds,
Upon black earth his white hoof pounds,
Over cold mountain streams he bounds
  And comes to a meadow mild;
There, when he kneels to take his nap,
He lays his head in a lady's lap
  As gently as a child.

WILLIAM JAY SMITH

Meeting

As I went home on the old wood road,
  With my basket and lesson book,
A deer came out of the tall trees
  And down to drink at the brook.

Twilight was all about us,
  Twilight and tree on tree;
I looked straight into its great, strange eyes
  And the deer looked back at me.

Beautiful, brown, and unafraid
  Those eyes returned my stare,
And something with neither sound nor name
  Passed between us there.

Something I shall not forget;
  Something still, and shy, and wise,
In the dimness of the woods,
  From a pair of gold-flecked eyes.

RACHEL FIELD

Moths and Moonshine

MOTHS and moonshine mean to me
Magic – madness – mystery.

Witches dancing weird and wild
Mischief make for man and child.

Owls screech from woodland shades,
Moths glide through moonlit glades,

Moving in dark and secret wise
Like a plotter in disguise.

Moths and moonshine mean to me
Magic – madness – mystery.

JAMES REEVES

5

I Wish, I Wish

The Petshop

If I had a hundred pounds to spend,
   Or maybe a little more,
I'd hurry as fast as my legs would go
   Straight to the Petshop door.

I wouldn't say, 'How much for this or that?'
   'What kind of a dog is he?'
I'd buy as many as rolled an eye,
   Or wagged a tail at me!

I'd take the hound with the drooping ears
   That sits by himself alone;
Cockers and Cairns and wobbly pups
   For to be my very own.

I might buy a parrot all red and green,
   And the monkey I saw before,
If I had a hundred pounds to spend,
   Or maybe a little more.

RACHEL FIELD

If I were a Queen

'IF I were a Queen,
What would I do?
I'd make you King,
And I'd wait on you.'

'If I were a King,
What would I do?
I'd make you Queen,
For I'd marry you.'

CHRISTINA ROSSETTI

If I Could Have a Pair of Wings

If I could have a pair of wings,
  Do you suppose that I
Would choose a pair of robin's wings
  And skim across the sky;
Or would I take the wings of gulls
  And glide across the seas;
Or would I buzz around the flowers
  With wings of busy bees?
I could, with wings of dragonflies,
  Dart over lakes and creeks;
Or with a pair of eagle's wings
  Soar over mountain peaks.
Perhaps, with wings of butterflies,
  I'd flutter out of sight;
But with mosquito wings, I guess,
  I'd flit about and bite.

ANITA E. POSEY

The Chickens

SAID the first little chicken
  With a queer little squirm,
'I wish I could find
  A fat little worm.'

Said the next little chicken
  With an odd little shrug,
'I wish I could find
  A fat little slug.'

Said the third little chicken
  With a sharp little squeal,
'I wish I could find
  Some nice yellow meal.'

Said the fourth little chicken
  With a small sigh of grief,
'I wish I could find
  A little green leaf.'

Said the fifth little chicken
  With a faint little moan,
'I wish I could find
  A wee gravel stone.'

'Now, see here,' said the mother,
  From the green garden patch,
'If you want any breakfast,
  Just come here and scratch.'

ANON.

In the Fashion

A LION has a tail and a very fine tail,
And so has an elephant, and so has a whale,
And so has a crocodile, and so has a quail –
    They've all got tails but me.

If I had sixpence I would buy one;
I'd say to the shopman, 'Let me try one';
I'd say to the elephant, 'This is *my* one.'
    They'd all come round to see.

Then I'd say to the lion, 'Why, *you've* got a tail!
And so has the elephant, and so has the whale!
And, look! There's a crocodile! *He's* got a tail!
    You've all got tails like me!'

A. A. MILNE

The Duck and the Kangaroo

SAID the Duck to the Kangaroo,
  'Good gracious! How you hop
Over the fields, and the water too,
  As if you never would stop!
My life is a bore in this nasty pond;
And I long to go out in the world beyond:
  I wish I could hop like you,'
  Said the Duck to the Kangaroo.

'Please give me a ride on your back,'
  Said the Duck to the Kangaroo:
'I would sit quite still, and say nothing but "Quack"
  The whole of the long day through;
And we'd go to the Dee, and the Jelly Bo Lee,
Over the land, and over the sea:
  Please take me a ride! Oh, do!'

Said the Kangaroo to the Duck,
  'This requires some little reflection.
Perhaps, on the whole, it might bring me luck:
  And there seems but one objection;
Which is, if you'll let me speak so bold,
Your feet are unpleasantly wet and cold,
  And would probably give me the roo –
  Matiz,' said the Kangaroo.

Said the Duck, 'As I sat on the rocks,
   I have thought over that completely;
And I bought four pairs of worsted socks,
   Which fit my web-feet neatly;
And to keep out the cold, I've bought a cloak;
And every day a cigar I'll smoke;
   All to follow my own dear true
   Love of a Kangaroo.'

Said the Kangaroo, 'I'm ready,
  All in the moonlight pale;
But to balance me well, dear Duck, sit steady,
  And quite at the end of my tail.'
So away they went with a hop and a bound;
And they hopped the whole world three times round,
  And who so happy, oh! who,
  As the Duck and the Kangaroo?

EDWARD LEAR

General Store

SOMEDAY I'm going to have a store
With a tinkly bell hung over the door,
With real glass cases and counters wide
And drawers all spilly with things inside.
There'll be a little of everything:
Bolts of calico; balls of string;
Jars of peppermint; tins of tea;
Pots and kettles and crockery;
Seeds in packets; scissors bright;
Bags of sugar, brown and white;
Biscuits and cheese for picnic lunches,
Bananas and rubber boots in bunches.
I'll fix the window and dust each shelf,
And take the money in all myself,
It will be my store and I will say:
'What can I do for you today?'

RACHEL FIELD

The Penny Fiddle

YESTERDAY I bought a penny fiddle
   And put it to my chin to play,
But I found that the strings were painted,
   So I threw my fiddle away.

If I had but saved up the halfpennies
   That I spent on buns and plums,
A shilling would have bought real music,
   But now the whisper comes.

I shall sell my boots to buy a fiddle,
   And walk about with ankles bare,
I shall laugh in the falling snow-flakes,
   For what should a fiddler care.

ROBERT GRAVES

The Swallow

Swallow, swallow, swooping free,
Do you not remember me?
I think last spring that it was you
Who tumbled down the sooty flue
With wobbly wings and gaping face,
A fledgling in the fireplace.

Remember how I nursed and fed you,
And then into the air I sped you?
How I wish that you would try
To take me with you as you fly.

OGDEN NASH

The Park

I OFTEN wish when lying in the dark,
Snug as a mouse,
In my bed at the top of the house,
I was still playing in the park,
Lying there upon the grass
Beneath the sky
Watching clouds go by
Like faces in a glass;
I do not ever need to sing
Myself to sleep,
Try my hand at counting sheep,
Instead I ride the night air in a swing;
A comet flashing through the dark,
I fall asleep in the park.

LEONARD CLARK

If I were Teeny Tiny

If I were teeny tiny
If I were teeny tiny
A mouse could be my pony
And we'd gallop very hard.

If I were tiny teeny
If I were tiny teeny
I would swim when it was rainy
In a puddle in the yard.

I would sleep inside a nut shell
It would make a handsome bed
With a petal for a pillow
To rest my little head.

I'd make dresses out of grasses
I'd weave slippers out of rushes
And instead of plates and glasses
I'd use leaves from off the bushes.

Oh the things that I would do
Are many many many
If I were teeny tiny
If I were teeny tiny.

BEATRICE SCHENK DE REGNIERS

When I Grow Up

WHEN I grow up,
I think I'll be
A detective
With a skeleton key.

I could be a soldier
And a sailor too;
I'd like to be a keeper
At the public zoo.

I'll own a trumpet
And I'll play a tune;
I'll keep a space ship
To explore the moon.

I'll be a cowboy
And live in the saddle;
I'll be a guide
With a canoe and a paddle.

I'd like to be the driver
On a diesel train;
And it must be fun
To run a building crane.

I'll live in a lighthouse
And guard the shore;
And I know I'll want to be
A dozen things more.

For the more a boy lives
The more a boy learns –
I think I'll be all of them
By taking turns.

WILLIAM WISE

Sitting Here

SITTING here
In our usual chairs
It's pleasant to think
Of polar bears,

Of polar bears
Amid ice-floes,
Dog sleds, and flat-faced
Eskimos.

It's pleasant to think,
On the other hand,
Of monkeys who live
In a tropical land,

And chatter and peer
At the forest floor
Where elephants stamp
And lions roar.

As high as the strong-winged
Eagles fly
Our little thoughts climb
To pierce the sky.

And deep in the sea
As fishes sink
A child may go
If a child will think.

High and low
And far and wide
Swift and nimble
A thought will ride,

But what it brings back
At the saddle bow,
Only the mind that sent it
Will know.

ELIZABETH COATSWORTH

6

A Knight and a Lady

A Knight and a Lady

A KNIGHT and a lady
  Went riding one day
Far into the forest,
  Away, away.

'Fair knight,' said the lady
  'I pray, have a care.
This forest is evil –
  Beware, beware!'

A fiery red dragon
  They spied on the grass;
The lady wept sorely,
  Alas! Alas!

The knight slew the dragon,
  The lady was gay.
They rode on together,
  Away, away.

ANON.

Teddy Bear

TEDDY was under the lilac bush –
when the snow went away, we found him there.
And one of his shoebutton eyes was lost
and the shine was gone from his yellow hair.
But Teddy blinked with his last black eye
and said that he really didn't care
(except that his cave was a trifle cold) . . .
as long as we came and found him there.
And he said with a smile on his white yarn mouth
that REAL bears slept in a cave or lair
all through the winter . . . and if they could,
well then, why couldn't a TEDDY bear?

AILEEN FISHER

Puppy and I

I MET a Man as I went walking;
We got talking,
Man and I.
'Where are you going to, Man?' I said
(I said to the Man as he went by).
'Down to the village to get some bread.
Will you come with me?' 'No, not I.'

I met a Horse as I went walking;
We got talking,
Horse and I.
'Where are you going to, Horse, today?'
(I said to the Horse as he went by).
'Down to the village to get some hay.
Will you come with me?' 'No, not I.'

I met a Woman as I went walking;
We got talking,
Woman and I.
'Where are you going to, Woman, so early?'
(I said to the Woman as she went by).
'Down to the village to get some barley.
Will you come with me?' 'No, not I.'

I met some Rabbits as I went walking;
We got talking,
Rabbits and I.
'Where are you going in your brown fur coats?'
(I said to the Rabbits as they went by).
'Down to the village to get some oats.
Will you come with us?' 'No, not I.'

I met a Puppy as I went walking;
We got talking,
Puppy and I.
'Where are you going this fine day?'
(I said to the Puppy as he went by).
'Up in the hills to roll and play.'
'I'll come with you, Puppy,' said I.

A. A. MILNE

Soldier, Soldier

'SOLDIER, soldier, won't you marry me,
    With your trumpet, fife and drum?'
'Oh no, sweet maid, I cannot marry you,
For I have no hat to put on.'

So up she went to her grandfather's chest,
And she got him a hat of the very, very best,
    And the soldier put it on!

'Soldier, soldier, won't you marry me,
    With your trumpet, fife and drum?'
'Oh no, sweet maid, I cannot marry you,
    For I have no coat to put on.'

So up she went to her grandfather's chest,
And she got him a coat of the very, very best,
    And the soldier put it on!

'Soldier, soldier, won't you marry me,
    With your trumpet, fife and drum?'
'Oh no, sweet maid, I cannot marry you,
    For I have no boots to put on.'

So up she went to her grandfather's chest,
And she got him a pair of the very, very best,
    And the soldier put them on!

'Soldier, soldier, won't you marry me,
    With your trumpet, fife and drum?'
'Oh no, sweet maid, I cannot marry you,
    For I have a wife of my own!'

ANON.

I Spy

As I went down the still woods
What should I see
But a mulberry and a medlar,
And a monkey up a tree.

As I went down the shady lane
What should I see
But a princess and a poacher,
And a place for tea.

As I went down the sandy shore
What should I see
But a crab and a crayfish
Coming up to me.

As I went down the steep street
What should I see
But a gay, grand gallant,
With a garter at his knee.

PAULINE CLARKE

I lost my mare in Lincoln Lane,
I'll never find her there again;
    She lost a shoe,
    And then lost two,
And threw her rider in the drain.

ANON.

Nine Red Horsemen

I SAW nine red horsemen ride over the plain,
And each gripped his horse by its long flowing mane.
  Ho-hillo-hillo-hillo-ho!

Their hair streamed behind them, their eyes were
    ashine,
They all rode as one man, although they were nine.
  Ho-hillo-hillo-hillo-ho!

Their spurs clinked and jingled, their laughter was gay,
And in the red sunset they galloped away.
  Ho-hillo-hillo-hillo-ho!

ELEANOR FARJEON

Extremely Naughty Children

By far
The naughtiest
Children
I know
Are Jasper
Geranium
James
And Jo.

They live
In a house
On the Hill
Of Kidd,
And what
In the world
Do you think
They did?

They asked
Their uncles
And aunts
To tea,
And shouted
In loud
Rude voices:
'We

Are tired
Of scoldings
And sendings
To bed:
Now
The grown-ups
Shall be
Punished instead.'

They said:
'Auntie Em,
You didn't
Say "Thank You"!'
They said:
'Uncle Robert,
We're going
To spank you!'

They pulled
The beard
Of Sir Henry
Dorner
And put him
To stand
In disgrace
In the corner.

They scolded
Aunt B.,
They punished
Aunt Jane;
They slapped
Aunt Louisa
Again
And again.

They said
'Naughty boy!'
To their
Uncle
Fred,
And boxed
His ears
And sent him
To bed.

Do you think
Aunts Em
And Loo
And B.,
And Sir
Henry
Dorner
(K.C.B.),

And the elderly
Uncles
And kind
Aunt Jane
Will go
To tea
With the children
Again?

ELIZABETH GODLEY

The Owl and the Pussy-Cat

THE Owl and the Pussy-Cat went to sea
   In a beautiful pea-green boat:
They took some honey, and plenty of money
   Wrapped up in a five-pound note.
The Owl looked up to the stars above,
   And sang to a small guitar,
'O lovely Pussy, O Pussy, my love,
   What a beautiful Pussy you are,
      You are,
      You are!
   What a beautiful Pussy you are!'

Pussy said to the Owl, 'You elegant fowl,
　　How charmingly sweet you sing!
Oh! let us be married; too long we have tarried:
　　But what shall we do for a ring?'
They sailed away, for a year and a day,
　　To the land where the bong-tree grows;
And there in a wood a Piggy-wig stood,
　　With a ring at the end of his nose,
　　　　His nose,
　　　　His nose,
With a ring at the end of his nose.

'Dear Pig, are you willing to sell for one shilling
    Your ring?' Said the Piggy, 'I will.'
So they took it away, and were married next day
    By the turkey who lives on the hill.
They dined on mince and slices of quince,
    Which they ate with a runcible spoon;
And hand in hand, on the edge of the sand,
    They danced by the light of the moon,
        The moon,
        The moon,
They danced by the light of the moon.

EDWARD LEAR

It's once I courted as pretty a lass,
   As ever your eyes did see;
But now she's come to such a pass,
   She never will do for me.
She invited me to her house,
   Where oft I'd been before,
And she tumbled me into the hog-tub,
   And I'll never go there any more.

ANON.

The Robber Kitten

A KITTEN once to its mother said:
  'I'll never more be good,
But I'll go and be a robber fierce,
  And live in a dreary wood,
    Wood, wood, wood,
And live in a dreary wood.'

So off it went to the dreary wood,
  And there it met a cock,
And blew its head, with a pistol, off,
  Which gave it an awful shock,
    Shock, shock, shock,
  Which gave it an awful shock.

Soon after that it met a cat.
  'Now, give to me your purse,
Or I'll shoot you through, and stab you too,
  And kill you, which is worse,
    Worse, worse, worse,
  And kill you, which is worse.'

It climbed a tree to rob a nest
  Of young and tender owls;
But the branch broke off, and the kitten fell
  With two tremendous howls,
    Howls, howls, howls,
  With two tremendous howls.

One day it met a Robber Dog,
    And they sat down to drink;
The dog did joke, and laugh and sing,
    Which made the kitten wink,
        Wink, wink, wink,
    Which made the kitten wink.

At last they quarrelled; then they fought,
    Beneath the greenwood tree,
Till puss was felled with an awful club,
    Most terrible to see,
        See, see, see,
    Most terrible to see.

When puss got up, its eye was shut,
    And swelled, and black and blue;
Moreover, all its bones were sore,
    So it began to mew,
        Mew, mew, mew,
    So it began to mew.

Then up it rose, and scratched its nose,
    And went home very sad:
'Oh mother dear, behold me here;
    I'll never more be bad,
        Bad, bad, bad,
    I'll never more be bad.'

                        R. M. BALLANTYNE

Three Jolly Huntsmen

THREE jolly huntsmen,
I've heard people say,
Went hunting together
On St David's Day.

All day they hunted,
And nothing could they find,
But a ship a-sailing,
A-sailing with the wind.

One said it was a ship,
The other he said, Nay;
The third said it was a house,
With the chimney blown away.

And all the night they hunted,
And nothing could they find
But the moon a-gliding,
A-gliding with the wind.

One said it was the moon,
The other he said, Nay;
The third said it was a cheese,
And half of it cut away.

And all the day they hunted,
And nothing did they find
But a hedgehog in a bramble-bush,
And that they left behind.

The first said it was a hedgehog,
The second he said, Nay;
The third said it was a pin cushion,
And the pins stuck in wrong way.

And all the night they hunted,
And nothing could they find
But a hare in a turnip-field,
And that they left behind.

The first said it was a hare,
The second he said, Nay;
The third said it was a calf,
And the cow had run away.

And all the day they hunted,
And nothing could they find
But an owl in a holly-tree,
And that they left behind.

One said it was an owl,
The second he said, Nay;
The third said 'twas an old man,
And his beard was growing grey.

ANON.

The Thief and the Shepherd

'Shepherdy, Shepherdy, count your sheep.'

'I can't come now, I'm fast asleep.'

'If you don't come now, they'll all be gone,
So Shepherdy, Shepherdy, come along.'

ANON.

Mine

I MADE a sand castle.
In rolled the sea.
    'All sand castles
    belong to me –
    to me,'
said the sea.

I dug sand tunnels.
In flowed the sea.
    'All sand tunnels
    belong to me –
    to me,'
said the sea.

I saw my sand pail floating free.
I ran and snatched it from the sea.
    'My sand pail
    belongs to me –
    to ME!'

LILIAN MOORE

Tea with me

A LITTLE brown bird looked in to see
What I was spreading on bread for tea.
He looked so hungry I felt I must
Eat the middle and leave him the crust.

The very next day he came again
Shivering cold in the pouring rain.
'I'm hungrier *still* today,' he said.
So I ate the crusts and gave him the bread.

Now every day, whatever the weather,
That sparrow and I have our tea-time together.
We chirrup and chatter like very old friends
And I eat the odds up while he eats the ends.

ALISON WINN

The Cats' Tea Party

FIVE little pussy-cats, invited out to tea,
Cried: 'Mother, let us go. Oh, do! for good we'll surely
    be.
We'll wear our bibs and hold our things as you have
    taught us how –
Spoon in right paws, cups in left – and make a pretty
    bow.
We'll always say, "Yes, if you please", and "Only half
    of that".'
'Then go, my darling children,' said the happy Mother
    Cat.

The five little pussy-cats went out that night to tea,
Their heads were smooth and glossy, their tails were
    swinging free;
They held their things as they had learned, and tried to
    be polite –
With snowy bibs beneath their chins they were a pretty
    sight.

But, alas, for manners beautiful, and coats as soft as silk!
The moment that the little kits were asked to take some
    milk,
They dropped their spoons, forgot to bow, and – oh,
    what do you think?
They put their noses in the cups and all began to drink!
Yes, every naughty little kit set up a miaou for more,
Then knocked the tea-cups over, and scampered
    through the door.

F. E. WEATHERLEY

Frog Went A-Courtin'

Mr Froggie went a-courtin' an' he did ride;
Sword and pistol by his side.

He went to Missus Mousie's hall,
Gave a loud knock and gave a loud call.

'Pray, Missus Mousie, air you within?'
'Yes, kind sir, I set an' spin.'

He tuk Miss Mousie on his knee,
An' sez, 'Miss Mousie, will ya marry me?'

Miss Mousie blushed an' hung her head,
'You'll have t'ask Uncle Rat,' she said.

'Not without Uncle Rat's consent
Would I marry the Pres-i-dent.'

Uncle Rat jumped up an' shuck his fat side,
To think his niece would be Bill Frog's bride.

Nex' day Uncle Rat went to town,
To git his niece a weddin' gown.

Whar shall the weddin' supper be?
'Way down yander in a holler tree.

First come in was a Bumble-bee,
Who danced a jig with Captain Flea.

Next come in was a Butterfly,
Sellin' butter very high.

An' when they all set down to sup,
A big gray goose come an' gobbled 'em all up.

An' this is the end of one, two, three,
The Rat an' the Mouse an' the little Froggie.

ANON.

7

One, Two, Three

1 AND 1 are 2 –
That's for me and you.

2 and 2 are 4 –
That's a couple more.

3 and 3 are 6
Barley-sugar sticks.

4 and 4 are 8
Tumblers at the gate.

5 and 5 are 10
Bluff seafaring men.

6 and 6 are 12
Garden lads who delve.

7 and 7 are 14
Young men bent on sporting.

8 and 8 are 16
Pills the doctor's mixing.

9 and 9 are 18
Passengers kept waiting.

10 and 10 are 20
Roses – pleasant plenty!

11 and 11 are 22
Sums for brother George to do.

12 and 12 are 24
Pretty pictures, and no more.

CHRISTINA ROSSETTI

Ten little chickadees sitting on a line,
One flew away and then there were nine.

Nine little chickadees on a farmer's gate,
One flew away and then there were eight.

Eight little chickadees looking up to heaven,
One flew away and then there were seven.

Seven little chickadees gathering up sticks,
One flew away and then there were six.

Six little chickadees learning how to dive,
One flew away and then there were five.

Five little chickadees sitting at a door
One flew away and then there were four.

Four little chickadees could not agree,
One flew away and then there were three.

Three little chickadees looking very blue,
One flew away and then there were two.

Two little chickadees sitting in the sun,
One flew away and then there was one.

One little chickadee living all alone,
He flew away and then there was NONE!

ANON.

Mice and Cat

ONE mouse, two mice,
Three mice, four,
Stealing from their tunnel,
Creeping through the door.

Softly! softly!
Don't make a sound –
Don't let your little feet
Patter on the ground.

There on the hearthrug,
Sleek and fat,
Soundly sleeping,
Lies old Tom Cat.

If he should hear you,
There'd be no more
Of one mouse, two mice,
Three mice, four.

So please be careful
How far you roam,
For if you should wake him . . .
He'd-chase-you-all-HOME!

CLIVE SANSOM

OLD Davy Jones had one little sailor,
Old Davy Jones had one little sailor,
Old Davy Jones had one little sailor,
    One little sailor boy.
He had one, he had two, he had three little sailors,
Four little, five little, six little sailors,
Seven little, eight little, nine little sailors,
    Ten little sailor boys.

Old Davy Jones had ten little sailors,
Old Davy Jones had ten little sailors,
Old Davy Jones had ten little sailors,
    Ten little sailor boys.
He had ten, he had nine, he had eight little sailors,
Seven little, six little, five little sailors,
Four little, three little, two little sailors,
    One little sailor boy.

ANON.

KNOCK, knock, knock, knock –
Hear the knockings four!
Each a knock for someone standing
At our kitchen door.

The first is a beggerman,
The second is a thief,
The third is a pirate,
And the fourth a robber chief.

Close all the windows,
Lock the door, and then
Call for the policeman quick
To catch those four bad men!

ANON.

Swinging on a gate, swinging on a gate,
Seven little sisters and a brother makes eight.
Seven pretty pinafores and one bow tie,
Fourteen pigtails and one black eye.

Swinging on a gate, swinging on a gate,
Seven little sisters and a brother makes eight.
Seven pretty ribbons and one little cap,
Eight books for school caught up in a strap.

Swinging on a gate, swinging on a gate,
Seven little sisters and a brother makes eight.
The school bell rings, and off they go –
Eight little children all in a row.

ANON.

ONE I love, two I love,
Three I love I say;
Four I love with all my heart,
Five I cast away.
Six he loves, seven she loves,
Eight they love together,
Nine he comes, ten he tarries,
Eleven he woos, and twelve he marries.

ANON.

Four Wrens

THERE were two wrens upon a tree,
Whistle and I'll come to thee;
Another came, and there were three,
Whistle and I'll come to thee;
Another came and there were four,
You needn't whistle any more,
For being frightened, off they flew,
And there are none to show to you.

ANON

CHOOK, chook, chook, chook, chook,
  Good morning, Mrs Hen.
How many chickens have you got?
  Madam, I've got ten.
Four of them are yellow,
  And four of them are brown,
And two of them are speckled red,
  The nicest in the town.

ANON.

ONE, two, kittens that mew,
Two, three, birds on a tree,
Three, four, shells on the shore,
Four, five, bees from the hive,
Five, six, the cow that licks,
Six, seven, rooks in the heaven,
Seven, eight, sheep at the gate,
Eight, nine, clothes on a line,
Nine, ten, the little black hen.

ANON.

My kitty-cat has nine lives,
Yes, nine long lives has she –
Three to spend in eating,
Three to spend in sleeping,
And three to spend up in the chestnut tree.

ANON.

Nine times nine,
The beetle's on the vine.
The cat is in the catmint.
And we're all quite fine.

Nine times nine,
The whale is in the brine,
A bigger fish is on the dish –
It's time for us to dine.

ANON.

I WENT fishing,
Took some bait.
Didn't go early,
Didn't go late.

Caught eight fishes
To put in my pail.
Seven were mackerel,
But the eighth was a whale.

The seven were easy
To put into the tin,
But that whale caused me trouble
Before I packed him in!

Took my catch home.
What did Mother say?
'Get those eight fish out of here –
We're having steak today!'

ANON.

TEN tom-toms,
Timpany, too,
Ten tall tubas
And an old kazoo.

Ten trombones –
Give them a hand!
The sitting-standing-marching-running
Big Brass Band.

ANON.

Coo

The dove says, '*Coo*,
  What shall I do?
It's hard, it's hard to keep my two.'
  'Pooh,' says the wren,
  'Why, I've got ten
And keep them all like gentlemen!'

ANON.

8

Stuff and Nonsense

My Name Is...

My name is Sluggery-wuggery
My name is Worms-for-tea
My name is Swallow-the-table-leg
My name is Drink-the-Sea.

My name is I-eat-saucepans
My name is I-like-snails
My name is Grand-piano-George
My name is I-ride-whales.

My name is Jump-the-chimney
My name is Bite-my-knee
My name is Jiggery-pokery
And Riddle-me-ree, and ME.

PAULINE CLARKE

Anna Elise

Anna Elise, she jumped with surprise;
The surprise was so quick, it played her a trick;
The trick was so rare, she jumped in a chair;
The chair was so frail she jumped in a pail;
The pail was so wet, she jumped in a net;
The net was so small, she jumped on the ball;
The ball was so round, she jumped on the ground;
And ever since then she's been turning around.

ANON.

From

Teapots and Quails

Teapots and Quails,
Snuffers and snails,
Set him a sailing
and see how he sails!

Mitres and beams,
Thimbles and Creams,
Set him a screaming
and hark! how he screams!

Ribands and Pigs,
Helmets and Figs,
Set him a jigging
and see how he jigs!

Tadpoles and Tops,
Teacups and Mops,
Set him a hopping
and see how he hops!

Lobsters and owls,
Scissors and fowls,
Set him a howling
and hark how he howls!

Eagles and pears,
Slippers and Bears,
Set him a staring
and see how he stares!

Sofas and bees,
Camels and Keys,
Set him a sneezing
and see how he'll sneeze!

Thistles and Moles,
Crumpets and Soles,
Set it a rolling
and see how it rolls!

Hurdles and Mumps,
Poodles and pumps,
Set it a jumping
and see how he jumps!

Pancakes and Fins,
Roses and Pins,
Set him a grinning
and see how he grins!

EDWARD LEAR

A Tale

There was an old woman sat spinning,
And that's the first beginning;
She had a calf,
And that's a half;
She took it by the tail,
And threw it over the wall,
And that's all.

ANON.

My Dream

I DREAMED a dream next Tuesday week,
　　Beneath the apple-trees;
I thought my eyes were big pork-pies,
　　And my nose was Stilton cheese.
The clock struck twenty minutes to six,
　　When a frog sat on my knee;
I asked him to lend me eighteenpence,
　　But he borrowed a shilling off me.

ANON.

Diddledy, Diddledy, Dumpty

DIDDLEDY, diddledy, dumpty;
The cat ran up the plum tree.
　　I'll wager a crown
　　I'll fetch you down;
Sing diddledy, diddledy, dumpty.

ANON.

American nursery rhymes

OLD Joe Brown, he had a wife,
    She was all of eight feet tall.
She slept with her head in the kitchen,
    And her feet stuck out in the hall.

*

WAY down yonder in the maple swamp
The wild geese gather and the ganders honk.
The mares kick up and the ponies prance;
The old sow whistles and the little pigs dance.

*

WHEN I am the President
    Of these United States,
I'll eat up all the candy
    And swing on all the gates.

*

JAY-BIRD, jay-bird, settin' on a rail,
Pickin' his teeth with the end of his tail;
Mulberry leaves and calico sleeves –
All school teachers are hard to please.

*

FUZZY WUZZY was a bear,
    A bear was Fuzzy Wuzzy.
When Fuzzy Wuzzy lost his hair
    He wasn't fuzzy, was he?

*

MIRROR, mirror, tell me,
    Am I pretty or plain?
Or am I downright ugly
    And ugly to remain?
Shall I marry a gentleman?
    Shall I marry a clown?
Or shall I marry old Knives and Scissors
    Shouting through the town?

*

THERE was an old owl who lived in an oak;
The more he heard, the less he spoke.
The less he spoke, the more he heard.
Why aren't we like that wise old bird!

Limericks

THERE was an Old Man on the Border,
Who lived in the utmost disorder;
    He danced with the Cat,
    And made Tea in his Hat,
Which vexed all the folks on the Border.

*

THERE was an old person of Dean
Who dined on one pea, and one bean;
    For he said, 'More than that,
    Would make me too fat,'
That cautious old person of Dean.

*

THERE was an Old Man, who when little
Fell casually into a Kettle;
    But, growing too stout,
    He could never get out,
So he passed all his life in that Kettle.

*

THERE was an Old Man of West Dumpet,
Who possessed a large Nose like a Trumpet;
    When he blew it aloud,
    It astonished the crowd,
And was heard through the whole of West Dumpet.

EDWARD LEAR

Dancing Game

MERRILY round and round he goes,
The Emperor's horse has silver hose;
Silver saddle and silver rein;
Merrily round we go again.
Hark, oh hark to the cackling hen:
Find me a husband, gentlemen,
The sun's too hot and the moon's too cold,
The clouds are too young and the stars too old.

HERE's my sister, and she can make
Pretty biscuits and plummy cake.
All the children are ill in bed,
Send them nothing but milk and bread.
Turn to the East and turn to the West,
A kiss for the one that you love the best.

ROSE FYLEMAN

from an Italian nursery rhyme

Strange Story

I SAW a pigeon making bread
I saw a girl composed of thread
I saw a towel one mile square
I saw a meadow in the air
I saw a rocket walk a mile
I saw a pony make a file
I saw a blacksmith in a box
I saw an orange kill an ox
I saw a butcher made of steel
I saw a penknife dance a reel
I saw a sailor twelve feet high
I saw a ladder in a pie
I saw an apple fly away
I saw a sparrow making hay
I saw a farmer like a dog
I saw a puppy mixing grog
I saw three men who saw these too
And will confirm what I tell you.

ANON.

*The secret of this poem is to stop in the middle of
each line*

If

If all the seas were one sea,
What a *great* sea that would be!
If all the trees were one tree,
What a *great* tree that would be!
And if all the axes were one axe,
What a *great* axe that would be!
And if all the men were one man,
What a *great* man that would be!
And if the *great* man took the *great* axe,
And cut down the *great* tree,
And let it fall into the *great* sea,
What a splish-splash that would be!

ANON.

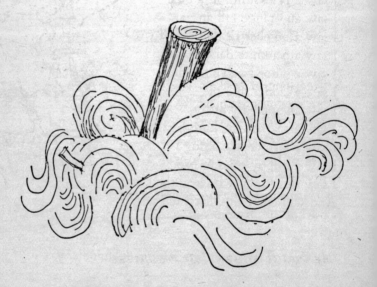

Sing a Song of Pockets

SING a song of pockets
A pocket full of stones
A pocket full of feathers
Or maybe chicken bones
A pocket full of bottle tops
A pocket full of money
Or if it's something sweet you want
A pocket full of honey . . .
ugh!

BEATRICE SCHENK DE REGNIERS

Jeremiah

JEREMIAH
Jumped in the fire.
Fire was so hot
He jumped in the pot.
Pot was so little
He jumped in the kettle.
Kettle was so black
He jumped in the crack.
Crack was so high
He jumped in the sky.
Sky was so blue
He jumped in a canoe.
Canoe was so deep
He jumped in the creek.
Creek was so shallow
He jumped in the tallow.
Tallow was so soft
He jumped in the loft.
Loft was so rotten
He jumped in the cotton.
Cotton was so white
He jumped all night.

ANON.

Index of First Lines

Index of Authors